REUBEN and the FIRE

P. BUCKLEY MOSS, Artist
Story by MERLE GOOD

Good Books
Intercourse, PA 17534
Printed in Mexico

Reuben and the Fire
Text copyright © 1993 by Merle Good
Art copyright © 1993 by P. Buckley Moss
Design by Dawn J. Ranck
International Standard Book Number: 1-56148-091-6
Library of Congress Catalog Card Number: 93-1798

Library of Congress Cataloging-in-Publication Data
Good, Merle.
    Reuben and the fire / P. Buckley Moss, artist ; text by
Merle Good.
        p. cm.
    Summary: Reuben, an Amish boy with five sisters,
witnesses the burning of a neighbor's barn and
experiences the excitement of the barnraising that
follows.
    ISBN 1-56148-091-6 : $14.95
    [1. Amish--Fiction. 2. Fires--Fiction.] I. Moss, P.
Buckley (Pat Buckley), 1933- ill. II. Title.
PZ7. G5998Re 1993
[E]--dc20   93-1798
                                                 CIP AC

Reuben knew that Annie was bossy. Oldest sisters often are. Reuben reached for the reins Annie held in her hands as they rounded the corner near Eli Lapp's mailbox. It was just the little pony cart they were in, after all, not the big buggy. There were groceries at their feet, Starshine trotting up ahead, evening coming.

"What gives?" Annie snapped, holding the leather lines tightly in her hand.

"Datt* lets me drive, Annie," he insisted.

"Oh, sure." That's what she always said. "Oh, sure." But when one of those ugly green buses tooted its horn and zipped around them with its awful smell, Reuben knew Annie would never give in.

Being the only boy with five sisters was just one of Reuben's problems. Trying to sneak across the fields to visit his friends, Ben and Sam, was tricky too.

"I'm going to help Mary in the garden," Annie said. "You carry the groceries in and then tie up the pony."

"She has a name, Annie."

"Oh, sure."

That's when Reuben got the idea. But he couldn't let Annie know.

Dawdi came over from his porch on the other side of the house. He was walking better and he was talking with excitement.
"Hopshine has babies," his grandfather smiled. Reuben couldn't believe it and took off like a hurricane for the old chicken house, Dawdi following as fast as he could.

Hopshine was Reuben's favorite rabbit. Reuben gave all of his animals names ending in "shine." His sisters laughed about the names, but he knew they were just jealous.

There were eight little baby rabbits. Dawdi loved little animals as much as he did.

"We're heading over to visit Gid Beiler," Datt was saying, leaning out from the buggy toward the chicken house door.

"How is Gid?" Dawdi asked.

Reuben's father shrugged. "He's feeling sick, I guess. Reuben, you get to bed on time if we're not back. We have to get the hay in tomorrow, if it's not too green."

Reuben nodded. Datt was ready to lift the reins when Mamm leaned over. "How many this time, Reuben?"

"Eight."

"Eight's a lot of shining," she smiled. Dawdi laughed as the buggy wheeled away and out the lane.

Reuben watched Dawdi walk back to the house. He saw Annie and Mary in the garden, but they were talking like big sisters always do.

Quickly, he slipped along the barn to where Starshine was tied. Instead of putting her in the barn, he was going to let her take him over to Ben and Sam. Unless Annie saw.

He sneaked around the back of the barn with Starshine, closing the fence, talking to the pony softly so she'd stay quiet. But just as he got to the back lane, his little sister Sadie stepped from the cornfield, smiling.

"I thought you were going to try something sneaky, little brother." She liked acting like she was older than Reuben.

"Please don't tell Annie." Too late.

"Annie!" Sadie shouted.

Reuben threw the reins to his little sister and took off, running down the lane. That would teach her not to tattle.

Ben and Sam were twins. They looked exactly the same. The only way Reuben could tell them apart was to check their ears. Sam's were smaller and smack against his head.

"I don't have older sisters," Ben was saying as they sat on the wall outside the cow stable. "But I know what a pest younger ones can be, especially Rachel."

That's when Sam noticed the cloud of smoke.

Reuben had never run so hard. It looked like the smoke was coming from his homeplace.

"I hope it's not our barn," he gasped to the twins as he ran, trying to see over the tops of the crops.

They saw the billowing smoke as they came over the ridge. The roof of a barn was burning.

"It's Abner Fisher's place," Sam said. The three of them stopped, staring at the frightening scene.

"We better go home and tell our parents," Sam said.

"Glad it's not our place," Reuben replied.

The twins nodded. "Yeah, but I feel sorry for Abner's family," Sam said. "I bet it's green hay."

Annie was hurrying out of the barn as Reuben came running around the corner. She looked upset.

"Can I go along over to the fire?" he asked.

"No way to treat your little sister," Annie grunted, pulling at the straps.

Reuben felt bad. He could see Sadie had been crying. "Sorry," he mumbled. Annie would never let him go along now, he was sure.

Wrong again. "Better get a fork and a shovel if you're going," she said. "But be quick."

It was hot and scary close to the fire. Neighbors were letting out the cows and horses.

"Can I help?" Reuben asked Abner.

"There are five little puppies in the milk house," Abner's oldest son answered. "See if someone can help you move them to the house. But be careful."

The fire was still at the other end of the big barn. Sam and Ben drove up with their father just in time to help Reuben carry the pups to the back porch of the house.

They could feel the heat of the fire as they ran, big eyes and droopy ears in their arms.

Reuben had never seen so many fire trucks. They came from everywhere, lights flashing red.

At first, everyone was afraid the house would burn too, but the firemen quickly sprayed water on it.

Two firemen had big colored pictures on their arms. Reuben had never seen such things close up before.

"They call them 'tattoos.' They do it by burning their skin," Sam said.

It was past midnight when Reuben crawled into bed. Dawdi had waited for them and wanted to hear all about the fire.

At first Reuben couldn't sleep, his mind full of flashing lights and smoke and tattoos. Then Mamm looked in on him and rubbed his forehead and his arm to help him relax. She was good that way.

Reuben dreamed that the puppies ran away on the fire truck.

Next morning Reuben could hardly stay awake during the milking. "Don't walk with your eyes closed," his sister Barbie complained.

At breakfast Datt announced the bad news. Reuben would have to stay home and bale the hay with Annie and Nancy.

"Cleaning up after a fire is no place for a young boy," Datt said. "Maybe you can go along to the barnraising tomorrow."

Mamm baked all day, with Barbie and Mary helping. A lot of food was needed for the barnraising. Reuben drove the horses and Annie and Nancy stacked the bales. Reuben was daydreaming, trying to name those eight little rabbits.

A barnraising is like a holiday. It seemed to Reuben that
everyone was there. His cousins from the southern end even came.
Ben and Sam brought their hammers, but they never got to
use them. All the boys could do was watch and run errands if they
were asked.

Big Henry Stoltzfus was the boss. Reuben liked him. By lunch the rafters were all in place. And the roof was going on before milking time.

"I'd like to be a carpenter like Big Henry," Sam said.

Ben laughed. "You better start growing."

Abner walked up to Datt and Reuben as they were leaving. He had one of the little pups in his arm. "Thanks for your help," he smiled. He looked tired.

"Gladly," Datt said. "We'll be back tomorrow if you can use us."

Abner smiled again. "Reuben, this puppy needs a home."

Reuben couldn't believe it. He looked at Datt, afraid he'd say no. But his father nodded with a smile.

"What'll you name him?" Abner asked. "I suppose Spotshine or some such name."

"Oh, no," Reuben exclaimed, taking the pup in his arms. "Can't you see the way his eyes shine?"

Riding home together in the carriage, his sisters giggled at the name. Datt was whistling softly under his breath. Mamm and Nancy had stayed to help serve the supper.

When they came to the covered bridge at the upper fork, Datt slowed the horses to a stop. "I'd like to tell Gid about the barnraising. It'll cheer him up. I'll be right home."

Datt crawled out of the buggy and handed the reins to Reuben. "Think you can manage?" he asked.

Reuben looked at his sister Annie. "Could you hold Eyeshine?" he asked her.

Annie looked at Datt, standing by the carriage, and then back at Reuben. "Why not," she said. "He's sorta cute, I think."

Barbie giggled again. The pup licked Annie's hand. Reuben smiled at Datt and took the reins. "Of course we can manage," he said. "See you at home."

Note

There are approximately 135,000 Old Order Amish persons, including children, living in 22 states and one province of North America. Reuben's family in this story is typical of the Amish in Lancaster County, Pennsylvania.

The religious beliefs of the Amish teach them to be cautious about many modern innovations such as automobiles, electricity, telephones, television, and higher education. They observe that these modern things often fragment people's lives and relationships more than they fulfill them. For 300 years, Amish communities have sought a "separate way," emphasizing family, honesty, basic values, and faith.

For more information about the Amish, write to or visit The People's Place, Route 340, Intercourse, PA 17534, an Amish and Mennonite heritage center (of which Merle Good and his wife Phyllis are Executive Directors). Or request a free list of books about the Amish.

About the Artist

P. Buckley Moss (Pat) first met the Amish in 1965 when she and her family moved to Waynesboro in the Shenandoah Valley of Virginia. Admiring the family values and work ethic of her new neighbors, Pat began to include the Amish in her paintings.

Many of her paintings and etchings of both the Amish and the Old Order Mennonites are displayed at the P. Buckley Moss Museum in Waynesboro, which is open to the public throughout the year. For more information, write to: The Director, P. Buckley Moss Museum, 2150 Rosser Avenue, Waynesboro, VA 22980.

About the Author

Merle Good has written numerous books and articles about the Amish, including the beautiful book *Who Are the Amish?* In addition to The People's Place, he and his wife Phyllis oversee a series of projects in publishing and the arts. They live in Lancaster, PA with their two daughters.